It's Christmas and Nina and Marcus' Birthday

Written by:
Harmel Deanne Codi, JD, MBA

Illustrated by:
Jewel Mason

It's Christmas and Nina and Marcus' Birthday

Copyright© 2020 by Harmel Deanne Codi, JD, MBA
Illustrated by: Jewel Mason

DEDICATION

To my children,
Jewel and Jodari – my source of
inspiration and drive.

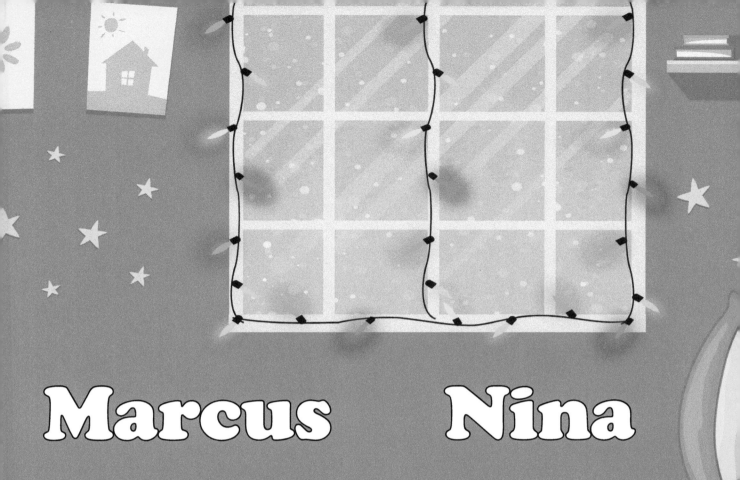

Marcus   Nina

5

"This Christmas tree is so huge," Marcus said, his eyes wide.

He and Nina had just awakened to find a large Christmas tree in the living room. There were boxes of decorations and Christmas lights all around.

8

They also heard Christmas songs coming from the kitchen.

"Hey, darlings, you know what tomorrow is, right?" Their Mommy, Jasmine, asked them.

"It's Christmas day!" Nina and Marcus shouted with excitement.

"Not just that," their Daddy, Clarence commented.

Nina and Marcus looked at each other. "It's also our birthday!" They screamed with excitement.

Nina and Marcus were born on Christmas day.

So tomorrow is going to be very special for them.

What makes this day even more special is that their Daddy just came back from military duties and will be here to celebrate it with them.

14

"That's right, tomorrow is your birthday, and it's also Christ's birthday. You'll be turning three. That means you both are very, very special," their Mommy said with a smile.

Later that evening, they all gathered around to decorate the Christmas tree.

"Daddy, I want to hang the star," Nina said when they were finished with hanging the rest of the decorations.

Her Daddy lifted her up and helped her hang the star.

Then they all stood back and admired the Christmas tree.

"It looks so colorful and beautiful with all the tinsel and lights," Nina exclaimed.

And, Marcus and Daddy agreed with a nod.

After dinner, they gathered for a Christmas story. Mommy handed out mugs of hot chocolate as their Daddy began the story.

"I'm going to tell you a story of a small fir tree that was ashamed of his height and size.

One day, all the big trees in the forest were chopped down to build ships.

The fir tree also wanted to be used to make the ships, but he was too small.

So, he was unhappy. Months later, a sparrow came and told him that the big trees would be decorated for Christmas. The small fir tree wanted to get decorated too.

And, one day, his wish came true. On Christmas Eve, the small fir tree was cut down and taken into a home not far from the forest. Inside the warm house, the parents and the children began to decorate the small tree.

He was decorated with small candles, toys, candy canes, and a gold star on top. The children loved the tree and talked about the candies and the toys placed around it.

Then, they sat down and listened to a man tell the Humpty-Dumpty's story. Soon, the fun was over, and everyone went to bed. The small fir tree was excited because he thought that the fun would continue the next morning. But he was wrong.

Instead of more fun, the servants of the house took the small tree to the storeroom. The small tree felt very sad and lonely. There, he saw a couple of mice that were really mean to him.

After some time, the nice fir tree was no longer pretty. He was dirty and brown. A young boy carried the little fir tree from the storeroom to the yard in the springtime. He thought that the family would dump him now. But he was wrong.

Finally, the little fir tree was replanted. He was so happy to be back in the forest with the other big trees. Suddenly, he understood that the little boy had taken him out there so he could live longer. Each and every year, the family dug him up again and decorated him with great love and care. He was thrilled to see his new family again. "The End"

By this time, the twins were feeling very sleepy, but they enjoyed the story very much.

"All right, time for bed, darlings," Their Mommy said as she led them to their bed.

The next morning, when Nina and Marcus woke up, two big cakes were on the table with their names written on them.

Then, the doorbell rang and when they opened the door – their grandparents, their aunties, uncles and their cousins brought them more Christmas and birthday gifts – Nina and Marcus were really excited.

Shortly after, it was time to unwrap all their gifts that the family bought for them. Nina had gotten a new Barbie doll, a dollhouse, new clothes, pink bicycle, and different colored hair bows.

Marcus had gotten new toy trucks, a ball, clothes, blue bicycle and wristwatch. They could not contend themselves as they kissed their Mommy and Daddy and the rest of the family to thank them.

Nina and Marcus had so much fun on their special day. They were glad that their birthday was on Christmas because their family made them very special by showering them with birthday and Christmas gifts.

About this Project

We are sincerely grateful that you choose to read our books to your child. It is an honor to bring this book series to the world and that all children will have more access to age-appropriate books to enjoy. This project was a long time coming, and we are thankful for all the support that undergird its arrival.

Early literacy is so critical in the lives of all children. The earlier children learn to read, brighter is their future. We hope that you continue to read for the child in your life as early as in utero. When we make reading and learning fun for kids, it becomes a wonderful hobby that opens a world of imagination and adventure.

We are so excited to bring this reading opportunity to all children, which is why all profits from our books' purchase go to our non-profit organization to encourage early literacy. We donate thousands of books yearly to our local pre-k and kindergarteners through our "My First Book Project." Your purchase opens access to donation of more books to children in our community that they too, can learn to read early. After all, we believe all readers are leaders

For more information on our non-profits and the community engagements, please visit: www.communityalliances.net

48

About the story line:

These books' ideas came to me while I was pregnant with my daughter Jewel (this book's illustrator) almost two decades ago. With both of my children, I started reading and singing for Jewel and my son Jodari once I discovered that I was pregnant. I knew that this would be the best gift that I could give them to propel them to a bright future as they become students and beyond. The years come quicker than I expected, and despite best efforts, I could not find time to get the books published. Then the pandemic happens, and we were all at home simultaneously, then Jewel and I started working on this project. Who would imagine that the books that were intended for them would be a gift to all children?

It has been an incredible journey to recreate these characters and bring these stories to our young readers. I am so grateful to my family that has partly inspired me to make this project a reality, and to each person who nudged me into embarking on this new endeavor. It has been a real joy.

About the Series
If you enjoy this book, please explore the entire series:
Mommy! Teach me how to read

Mommy! Teach me How to Count

Mommy! Teach me How to Sing

Mommy! Teach me How to Play

Mommy! Teach me How to Write

Mommy! Teach me How to Pray

Mommy! Teach me How to Dance

Daddy is home from Military

Daddy , Teach me how to ride Bicycle

Daddy, Teach me how to swim

Daddy , Teach me how to tie my shoelace

CPSIA information can be obtained
at www.ICGtesting.com
Printed in the USA
BVHW010038100223
658265BV00008B/314

9 781736 077757